To the parents who kept asking me to write a book to help their children. I pray that your sons and daughters learn from their losses and become winners, regardless of circumstances. And thank you to Audrey Moralez and Charlie Wetzel for helping me write this book.

— *J.M.*

For kids who try, even when they're scared. That's brave.

— *S.B.*

The illustrations for this book were done in pen and ink and watercolor on watercolor paper. The text was set in Bookman Old Style, and the display type is Berthold Baskerville. This book was edited by Pam Gruber and designed by Patti Ann Harris, Phil Caminiti, Aram Kim, and Gene Vosough. The production was supervised by Erika Schwartz, and the production editor was Andy Ball.

John C. Maxwell

Sometimes You Win Sometimes You Learn

For Kids!

Illustrations by Steve Björkman

Little, Brown and Company
New York   Boston

Welcome to Woggletown, a bustling place,
Where kids play together in green, open space.
They romp and they race and they jump and they spin,
For Woggles—like most kids—really love to win.

Meet brother and sister Wendy and Wade,
Who have finally reached Woggleball age.
Wade is the short one, he's funny and loud.
Wendy is tall and stands out in a crowd.

They both want to win, so to Papa they go.
He's old and he's wise and he'll certainly know.
"Let's ask him!" "Let's visit!" they both start to say.
They jump on their scooters and zoom on their way.

"Papa, please tell us the secret to winning!"
He hugs them both tight, and says while he's grinning,
"All's well that begins well. Keep hope in your heart.
Think positive thoughts—that's how all winners start."

Woggleball looks simple when you first see the sport.
The court is not long and the baskets are short.
It seems to be easy but of course it is not.
There is no way to win without a positive thought.

The other team's mighty and soon gains the lead.
They outmatch the Woggles in skill and in speed.
Wendy starts dragging, and says, "This isn't fun!"
She gives up hope before the game's even done.

Papa finds the kids grumpy after the game.
Wade kicks at the dirt while Wendy complains.
But Papa won't have it. He says, *"When you're through,
I have winning wisdom I'd like to give you."*

They all go for ice cream and that does the trick.
Wade and Wendy feel better—their mood's over quick.
Papa gives them a hug. He's no longer stern.
"Get rest, and tomorrow we'll take time to learn."

"Too often we're angry when things don't go right.
Let go of your loss. Yesterday ended last night.
The first step to take in a winning direction
Is to work on yourself with an attitude correction.

"Woggles are winners, yes, that much is true.
But whether you win depends upon YOU.
Winning takes effort, this much you will see.
What you learn from your loss can bring victory!"

Wade turns toward Wendy and they start to smile.
Their attitudes have already changed by a mile.
Wade says, "Be positive. That's what we'll do!
But what else, Papa? Will you give the next clue?"

"Just take it inch by inch and then yard by yard.
If you win in small steps, it's not quite as hard."

In the very next game, they run fast and play strong.
Wade dodges and jumps, and yells, "Wendy, go long!"
The Woggletown team tries with all of their might,
But in the end it's the same. They lose the fight.

After the game, the kids are tired but proud,
And they smile as they walk, high-fiving the crowd.
Wendy and Wade say to Papa together,
"We didn't win, but at least we got better!"

"When things don't go well and a loss comes your way,
The question to ask is: 'Did I learn today?'
Always do your best, then stretch to get better.
Go further, go further—be a go-getter!

"So, when things are harder than at first they may seem,
It's improvement that matters most to a team.

"Woggles are winners, yes, that much is true.
But whether you win depends upon YOU.
Winning takes effort, this much you will see.
What you learn from your loss can bring victory!"

The kids want to improve, so they work extra hard.
They're shooting and passing and learning to guard.
Practice is tiring, but as Papa would say,

"Winning takes work—it's uphill all the way.
Quitting's for quitters and they never win.
A loss is a loss till you make it a win."

Game day is here! The whole team is ready.
The opponents are good, but the Woggles hold steady.
It's a close match, and the kids never quit.
Wade reminds Wendy, "Try to win bit by bit!"

The kids hustle and bustle and then take the lead.
The Woggles are smaller but they surely have speed.
One second is left...then a cheer from the crowd!
Wendy and Wade see their papa is proud.

We all like to win. Yes, that much is true.
But whether you win depends upon YOU.
Take this lesson to heart, and say with a grin,
Sometimes you learn, and sometimes you win.

A NOTE TO YOU FROM PAPA

I love asking two questions of Wendy and Wade,
To teach them to think—what a difference it's made.
Since you've finished this story, now it's your turn.
Tell me:

"What did you love? And what did you learn?"

Dear Parent,

One of the most important things you can do for children is to help them understand that life is made up of highs and lows, successes and failures. And it's important to know how to positively handle setbacks when they do come.

I was fortunate to learn these lessons from my parents, Melvin and Laura Maxwell. My father continually challenged me to get back up whenever I got knocked down, to learn from my mistakes, and to keep trying—all while maintaining a positive attitude. My mother gave me the security of knowing that no matter what I did wrong or how badly I messed up, she was going to support my next attempt and keep on loving me unconditionally.

My wife, Margaret, and I have tried to pass these lessons on to our two children. Now we're teaching them to our five grandchildren. And nothing would please us more than helping people like you to pass them on to your children.

Read the story with your children. Ask questions about the difficulties they are experiencing. Share how you've learned from your mistakes, and how that helped you succeed afterward. Encourage your children to learn how to win bit by bit. And most important, reassure them that, whether they win or lose, you will always love them unconditionally.

Your friend,

John C Maxwell